WATCH
CORN GROW

By Kristen Rajczak

Gareth Stevens
Publishing

Please visit our Web site, www.garethstevens.com. For a free color catalog of all our high-quality books, call toll free 1-800-542-2595 or fax 1-877-542-2596.

Library of Congress Cataloging-in-Publication Data

Rajczak, Kristen
Watch corn grow / Kristen Rajczak.
    p. cm. — (Watch plants grow!)
ISBN 978-1-4339-4823-7 (pbk.)
ISBN 978-1-4339-4824-4 (6-pack)
ISBN 978-1-4339-4822-0 (library binding)
1. Corn—Growth—Juvenile literature. 2. Corn—Development—Juvenile literature. I. Title.
QK495.G74M36555 2011
633.1'5—dc22

                                        2010039140

First Edition

Published in 2011 by
Gareth Stevens Publishing
111 East 14th Street, Suite 349
New York, NY 10003

Copyright © 2011 Gareth Stevens Publishing

Editor: Kristen Rajczak
Designer: Haley W. Harasymiw

Photo credits: Cover, pp. 1, 3, 5, 7, 9, 11, 13, 15, 17, 19, 23 Shutterstock.com; p. 21 Wrangel/iStockphoto.com.

Printed in the United States of America

CPSIA compliance information: Batch #CW11GS: For further information contact Gareth Stevens, New York, New York at 1-800-542-2595.

WATCH
CORN GROW

See the rows of corn.

Corn plants are called stalks.

Corn plants have long leaves.

Corn grows under the leaves.

Corn plants have silk.

13

The silk turns brown.
Then the corn is picked.

Corn is yellow, white, or blue.

Corn seeds are called kernels.

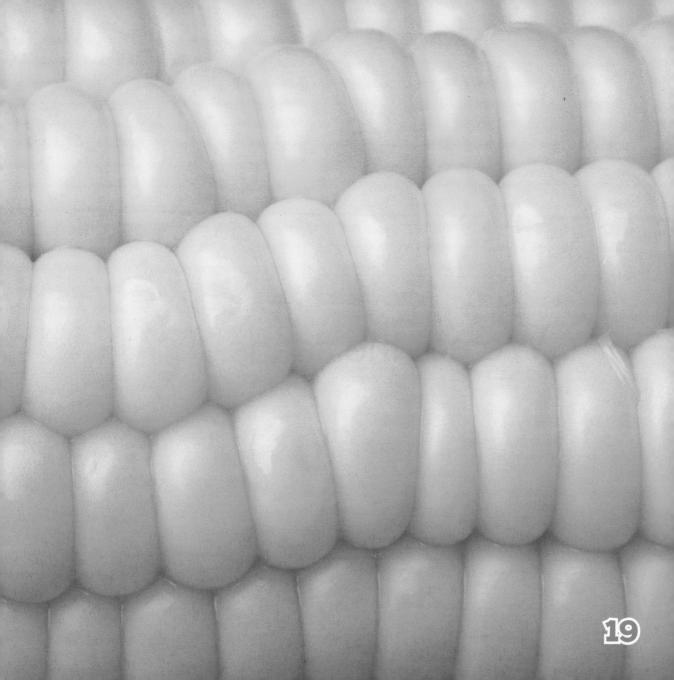

We eat the seeds.

21

Chickens eat them, too!

Words to Know

kernels

silk

stalk